McMillen
790 L

Natural Habitat

Also by Anna Branford
Violet Mackerel's Brilliant Plot
Violet Mackerel's Remarkable Recovery

VIOLET MACKEREL'S

Natural Habitat

Anna Branford

illustrated by
Elanna Allen

A
atheneum
Atheneum Books for Young Readers
New York   London   Toronto   Sydney   New Delhi

Atheneum Books for Young Readers

An imprint of Simon & Schuster Children's Publishing Division
1230 Avenue of the Americas, New York, New York 10020

ATHENEUM BOOKS FOR YOUNG READERS is a registered trademark of
Simon & Schuster, Inc.
Atheneum logo is a trademark of Simon & Schuster, Inc.
For information about special discounts for bulk purchases, please
contact Simon & Schuster Special Sales at 1-866-506-1949 or
business@simonandschuster.com.
The Simon & Schuster Speakers Bureau can bring authors to your live event.
For more information or to book an event, contact the Simon & Schuster
Speakers Bureau at 1-866-248-3049 or visit our website at
www.simonspeakers.com.
Also available in an Atheneum Books for Young Readers paperback edition.
Book design by Lauren Rille
The text for this book is set in Excelsior.
The illustrations for this book are rendered in pencil with digital ink.
Manufactured in the United States of America
0413 FFG
First US Edition
10 9 8 7 6 5 4 3 2 1
Library of Congress Cataloging-in-Publication Data
Branford, Anna.
Violet Mackerel's natural habitat / Anna Branford ;
illustrated by Elanna Allen. — 1st US ed.
p. cm.
Summary: As the youngest in her family, seven-year-old Violet identifies with small creatures in the natural world, but when she tries to help a special ladybug, she learns an important lesson about animal habitats.
ISBN 978-1-4424-3594-0 (hardcover : alk. paper)
ISBN 978-1-4424-3595-7 (pbk. : alk. paper)
ISBN 978-1-4424-3596-4 (eBook : alk. paper)
[1. Family life—Fiction. 2. Ladybugs—Fiction. 3. Habitat (Ecology)—Fiction.]
I. Allen, Elanna, ill. II. Title.
PZ7.B737384Vh 2013
[Fic]—dc23   2012015000

For Gaynor
(my mama)
—A. B.

Mumma, I drew this for you.
Will you put it up on the fridge?
—E. A.

Natural Habitat

1

The Indoor Sparrow

Violet Mackerel is a seven-year-old girl who is at the shopping center with her mama.

They have been there all afternoon, buying violin strings for Violet's eleven-year-old brother, Dylan, and an *Encyclopedia of Natural Science* for her thirteen-year-old sister, Nicola, who is doing a special display for a school science fair. They have not been buying anything for Violet, unless you count gray school socks. Violet does not count gray school socks.

And now Mama has bumped into Mrs. Lin from across the road and they are having an extremely long cup of tea in the food court.

"With petrol prices as they are," says Mama to Mrs. Lin, "it's getting difficult to make ends meet."

"I know," says Mrs. Lin to Mama. "My bills are going through the roof."

No one says anything to Violet, so she thinks about Mrs. Lin's bills going through the roof. The roof of the food court is quite high up. Past two whole floors of shops. And there is a small brown sparrow flying there.

Violet wonders if the sparrow has always lived in the shopping mall or if he flew in by mistake

and can't find his way out of the automatic sliding doors that creak open and shut as the people come and go. She wonders if indoor sparrows are jealous of outdoor sparrows, who have leafy trees to nest in, or if outdoor sparrows are jealous of indoor sparrows, who get doughnut crumbs and bits of hot dog to eat. It is difficult to know what small creatures think. But while Violet is wondering, the sparrow flies down onto the floor of the food court and hops and jumps just near where she is sitting.

Violet wishes she had some doughnut crumbs, but since she doesn't, she tries to think of what else a sparrow might like. She suspects it is probably quite difficult for an indoor sparrow to find things to build a nest with, and that gives her an idea. The hem of her daisy skirt is coming unraveled, and she pulls on a loose thread. It gets quite long before it breaks. Violet puts it down on the ground for the sparrow.

"You can weave this into your nest," says Violet.

The sparrow hops over, picks it up in his beak, and flies back toward the roof of the shopping mall.

Violet smiles. A new thought is forming in her mind. It is called the Theory of Helping

Small Things and it works like this:
If you do something to help a small
thing, that small thing might find a
way of helping you.

Violet waits to see if anything
happens.

The sparrow flies back down
again and this time it hops and
jumps near Mrs. Lin's feet. Mrs. Lin
wrinkles her nose.

"Ugh, I can't stand
sparrows. They look
like mice with wings,"

8

says Mrs. Lin. "It's time I was going home."

"Us too, I suppose," says Mama.

"Thank you," whispers Violet to the sparrow, very glad that they are finally leaving.

In the car Violet asks Mama about birds who live in shopping centers.

"Birds are good at finding places to build their nests and things to eat wherever they are," says Mama, "but a shopping center is not a bird's natural habitat."

"What's a natural habitat?" asks Violet.

"The place where something lives and grows best," says Mama.

Violet suspects that the shopping center is not her natural habitat either.

The Small Ladybug

When they get home, Mama gets busy cooking dinner and everyone is talking about Nicola's natural science project. Violet thinks it is the perfect time to test her new theory a bit more.

In her garden there is a patch of fennel with soft, feathery leaves. Lots of ladybugs live in it, and one of them is a bit smaller than the others.

Violet wonders what sort of help a small ladybug might like.

The trick of *helping* small things, Violet suspects, is to *understand* them.

Violet is the smallest in her family, so she expects she knows how the small ladybug feels. It probably has to go to bed before all the others, and whenever it finds out something interesting (like that your ears keep growing all your life, even when you are old), the bigger ladybugs probably say they already knew.

Violet gently nudges the small ladybug onto the tip of her finger. She names it Gloria. Naming is not exactly understanding *or* helping but it is a good start, she thinks.

Small Gloria sits on Violet's fingertip for a little while in a friendly way. Violet tells her about her big sister, Nicola, (who is always grumpy these days) and her big brother, Dylan, (who is going through a stage). Then she puts Small Gloria back into the feathery fennel plant.

Violet goes inside to think of a plan for helping Small Gloria, but it is hard to think properly because there is so much crossness coming from the kitchen.

"Everyone else has something interesting for their natural science project," Nicola is saying to Mama. "Anson McGregor is building an ant farm and Nigel Ridley is growing blue crystals and Belinda Maxwell has a real Venus flytrap plant and she will be feeding it flies with tweezers for the fair."

"Well, I'm sure you can do something

interesting for your project too,"
says Mama. "What would you *like* to
do?"

But Nicola does not know, and
that is the problem. She says natural
science is her worst subject. She says

it is worse than math, much worse. She says she does not see the *point* in rediscovering something that has already been discovered and then making a display of it.

"Maybe you could discover things about ladybugs that *haven't* been discovered yet," says Violet helpfully. "There are lots in the garden."

Violet says this quite loudly so that Mama will notice how helpful she is being. Mama is probably thinking, If only everyone was as helpful as Violet and always had such good ideas. She is probably thinking of a special treat for Violet as a thank-you for always being such a help to everybody.

Nicola, however, is not thinking of Violet's helpfulness.

"Buzz off, Violet," she says. "It's not an elementary-school project where you can just put some lady-bugs in a jar. It is for a fair, and it has to be actual *science*."

"Nicola," says Mama, "Violet is only trying to help."

Violet sighs deeply with the wounded look of someone who has been buzzed off while only trying to help. She stares at the ground for a long time in sad silence. Nicola is probably wishing she could take it back. Mama is probably thinking that a good treat for poor, helpful, buzzed-off Violet would be her own kitten.

Although actually,

when Violet looks up, Mama and Nicola have gone back to reading the *Encyclopedia of Natural Science.*

So Violet takes a glass jar from the kitchen cupboard. Nicola might not have any ideas for herself, but she has given one to Violet.

3
The
New
Habitat

It is drizzling now, and one of Violet's favorite feelings is to be warm and dry inside while there is wetness and coldness blowing around outside. The fennel patch probably isn't very cozy for a small ladybug on a rainy day. Cold wind and raindrops would easily sneak through the feathery leaves. So Violet decides to help Small Gloria by making her a *new* habitat, which will be nicer than her natural one.

Gloria likes fennel, so Violet snips some from the plant outside and puts that in the jar first. Violet likes Christmas tinsel, and she has some that she saved from Christmas, so she puts that in next. There are sweet pea flowers in a jug on the kitchen table that Mama's boyfriend,

Vincent, gave her. Mama doesn't mind Violet having one, so she puts it in with the tinsel. All living creatures need water, so she sprinkles a little bit in with her fingertips. And then Violet makes a paper sign for the new home, which says NEW HABITAT OF

SMALL GLORIA. She sticks it onto the jar with sticky tape.

It is a good habitat, Violet thinks, but it needs something else— something ladybugs really like, so that when a smallish ladybug has one, the bigger ladybugs all wish they had one too. Violet has a wishing stone she was given at a fairy party. It is a small, clear pebble with a rainbow glaze, and it is a particular treasure of hers. She puts it very carefully in the jar, on top of the fennel but underneath the silver

tinsel. And now the New

Habitat of Small

Gloria is ready.

Violet takes

her umbrella and

the jar out into the garden. The trou-

ble with small things is that they

can be the hardest to spot, especially

in the half-light of evening. Violet

looks closely into the fennel patch.

At first she can't see any ladybugs

at all. Then after a while of standing

over the patch and sheltering it with her umbrella, she can see some of the bigger ones scurrying about as raindrops drip through the feathery leaves. But the small ladybug is nowhere to be seen.

Violet looks right in the middle of the plant, near the stalk, to see if it is sheltering there. Then she tries looking out at the very tips, in case it is stuck where the leaves have been bouncing up and down the most. She walks in a circle around the fennel, just to make sure she hasn't missed a spot. But she cannot find the small ladybug anywhere.

Just as she is about to give up and go back inside, she has the idea of looking among some pebbles that she and Nicola used to build a ladybug cave under the fennel leaves last summer. It was quite a secret place, which Nicola and Violet used for hiding small notes they wrote to each other, a bit like a private letter box. That was before everything made Nicola grumpy, especially Violet. Now the cave has fallen down, but the pebbles are still there in a little heap. Violet carefully lifts them one by one to avoid squashing any small creature underneath. And there, right at the bottom of the pile between two pebbles, she spies a ladybug that is a bit smaller than the others and

sort of looks up if you say "Small Gloria."

Violet gently nudges the little ladybug onto her finger, puts her finger against the silver tinsel in the jar, and lets Small Gloria explore the new habitat. Gloria walks carefully down the tinsel and around the wishing stone, which is nearly twenty times as big as she is. She looks at her reflection in it for a while, and then disappears into the fennel.

So that Small Gloria doesn't accidentally fly out and lose her new habitat, Violet puts the lid on the jar. She walks with it very carefully, so that there is not too much joggling, and takes it upstairs to her room.

Then it is dinnertime, and it is cheese-on-toast. Violet saves a corner for Gloria.

That night Violet says good night to Nicola, who is still grumpy. Then she says good night to Dylan, who says, "Is it?," which Mama says is part of the stage he is going through. Then she says good night to Vincent and to Mama. And then, just before bed, she gently opens the lid of the New Habitat of Small Gloria.

She puts in the dinner she has saved.

"Good night, Small Gloria," she says.

Violet puts her ear over the
mouth of the jar, in case there is any
sort of reply, but there is none, which
is normal for ladybugs. Violet feels
she might be getting quite good at
understanding small things.

Violet puts the lid back on, puts the jar on her bedside table, and tries to go to sleep, but it is difficult when there is a new friend in your room.

In the morning it will be just her and Nicola, since Mama and Vincent and Dylan are all going to the market very early. Mama has a stall to sell knitted things, Vincent has a stall selling china birds, and Dylan plays his violin and people throw coins into his violin case. Usually Nicola and Violet go too, so Nicola can sell the earrings she makes out of beads and Violet can help everybody and also eat little pancakes out of a paper cup.

But tomorrow Nicola will be working on her project and Violet plans to stay home too, for the pretend reason of sleeping in, but for the *actual* reason of Small Gloria.

4 The Horrible Morning

In the morning Violet has the feeling of something exciting that you can't quite remember for the first few seconds while you are waking up. And then she spies the jar on her bedside table, and she remembers.

Violet picks it up and looks inside, turning it slowly and gently so that its resident doesn't get queasy. But she cannot see Small Gloria.

She undoes the lid and looks inside.

Violet takes out the corner of cheese-on-toast, which does not seem very nibbled, and carefully pulls out the silver tinsel, in case Gloria is hiding there. Then, very gently, she tweaks out the feathery fennel.

In the bottom of the jar there are only two things left.

One is the wishing stone.

The other is Gloria, the wrong way up and not moving, with her legs curled tightly against her.

Violet feels a bit queasy, as though *her* habitat is being turned around. The ladybug is not walking or flying or even looking up a bit when Violet says "Small Gloria." She is just lying quite still on her back beside the wishing stone.

Violet is not sure what to do.

It is a horrible surprise.

She sits still on her bed for a little while and

wishes Mama would come home. She would like to tell someone what has happened, even though they might just say, "It's only a ladybug" or "That wasn't very clever to put it in a jar." But there is only grumpy Nicola. This morning, of all mornings, Violet does not feel like being buzzed off.

Violet stands in Nicola's doorway with the jar in her hand. Nicola is sitting at her desk, still looking through the *Encyclopedia of Natural*

Science. She has the look of someone who has not been to sleep yet.

"Nicola?" says Violet.

"What?" grumps Nicola.

Violet thinks of how the problem of Small Gloria is much more horrible than the problem of the natural science project and feels slightly cross as well as sad.

Then suddenly Nicola's face goes

a bit funny, like she is trying not to sneeze. Then she does a strange cough. And then she starts crying. Nicola doesn't cry very often, and when she does, it is usually like a grown-up, just tears and sniffling and not much noise.

This different way of crying is another bad surprise for the morning.

Violet is not supposed to go into Nicola's room without knocking, and after she knocks she is supposed to wait until Nicola says, "Come in," because of an incident a few weeks ago that involved some borrowed nail polish and a spillage. But this morning Violet just goes in and holds Nicola's hand.

"Are you sad about your project?" asks Violet after a little while.

Nicola nods and gulps. "I can't do it," she says.

"It does sound difficult," says Violet, even though there is no one around to think of giving her a kitten.

"Only to a pea brain like me," says

Nicola with a hiccup. "Everyone will laugh at me at the natural science fair."

"You're not a pea brain," says Violet. "*I'm* the pea brain," she adds.

"Why are you a pea brain?" Nicola sniffs.

"I tried to make a new habitat for Small Gloria, so she wouldn't always have to be out in the cold and wet," says Violet, "and now look."

Violet shows Nicola the jar with the wishing stone and the little upside-down ladybug.

Nicola does not say "So what, it's just a ladybug," and she also does not say "It wasn't very clever to put it in a jar." It is nice, when two people are having disasters, if neither of them says anything like that.

Violet pulls up a chair at Nicola's desk, where the *Encyclopedia of Natural Science* is still open.

"Maybe we can be pea brains together," says Violet.

5 The Possible Idea

"I was reading last night about the life spans of animals," says Nicola a bit later, looking it up in the encyclopedia. "Ladybugs don't live for very long. Mostly, the bigger the animal, the longer it lives, and the smaller the animal, the shorter it lives."

Blue whales, which are the biggest animals, can live for ninety years, reads Violet from the

encyclopedia, *but mayflies, which are very tiny, live only for a few hours.*

Violet is quite glad she is a person and not a mayfly or she would have

had all her life in the shopping mall yesterday while Mama had tea with Mrs. Lin.

"How long do ladybugs live?" asks Violet.

"I'm not sure exactly," says Nicola, "but I think maybe Gloria would have had quite a short life even if she had stayed in her natural habitat. I don't think it's all your fault."

Violet wishes Gloria was alive in

the fennel patch and not dead in the bottom of a jar, but it is nice to think that it might not be all her fault.

"Maybe the jar was not a good habitat for a ladybug," says Violet.

"Maybe not," says Nicola, but not meanly.

Although she is extremely sad, Violet thinks it is nice with just the two of them there, sitting at the desk in her sister's room, not being told to buzz off. She is glad that she and Nicola share the same habitat.

Violet looks up ladybugs in the encyclopedia. There is a picture of their life cycle, which starts with lots of tiny yellow eggs sitting on a leaf. They look like the little yellow seed beads Nicola sometimes uses when she is making earrings, and that gives Violet a possible idea.

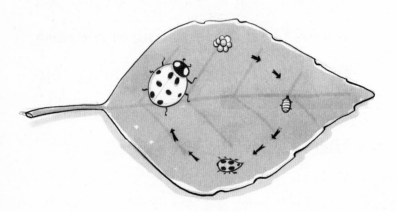

"You could make that out of green felt and yellow seed beads," she says.

Once at Christmastime, Nicola made little dangling elves with hats out of beads, and some were holding presents and some were holding candy canes. Even though Violet helped to pack up most of the Christmas decorations, she quite liked the elf and still has it on the windowsill of her bedroom. Eggs on a leaf are easy compared with that.

"Everyone else has real living things in their display," says Nicola.

"Maybe you could make a special sign to say that you made yours out of beads because it is better for real living things to be in their natural habitats," suggests Violet. "And anyway, the things you make are as beautiful as real things."

Nicola smiles and says, "Thanks, Violet."

Nicola looks thoughtfully at the encyclopedia's life cycle of the ladybug. "It would be a lot of work to make all those different stages out of beads and things," she says.

"But I could help you," says Violet.

"Thanks," says Nicola again.

Between Mama's basket of scraps, Nicola's collection of jewelry-making supplies, and Violet's box of small things, they collect everything that they need to re-create the life cycle of the ladybug. Then they get to work. Violet holds a real leaf very still while Nicola traces around it to get its shape on the green felt. Nicola cuts it out and stitches on tiny yellow seed beads in little clusters while Violet passes her useful things, like scissors and thread.

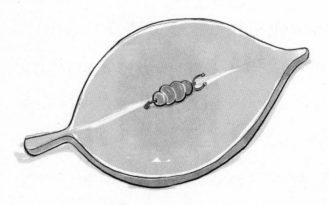

Violet has not forgotten Small Gloria, who must once have been inside a tiny yellow egg on a leaf. She wonders if Gloria knew she was actually trying to help her. Violet still wishes she could help Gloria, but since she can't, she is glad that she can help Nicola.

6 The Beaded Life Cycle

With Violet doing so much helping, the first stage of the ladybug's life cycle is ready quite quickly. While Nicola is sewing on the very last tiny yellow seed bead, Violet reads to her from the encyclopedia.

"'Ladybugs lay their eggs on leaves in groups of ten to fifty. They are laid as close as possible to an aphid colony, since ladybugs like to eat aphids.'"

It is funny to think that Small Gloria would probably have pre-ferred a spindly green aphid to cheese-on-toast, Violet thinks, but that is the way of ladybugs and no

wonder it is hard to understand them. Using one of Nicola's special gel pens, which would not usually be allowed, Violet draws a green aphid colony to go near the felt leaf.

"'Next is the larva stage, which is when the eggs hatch and long, thin gray-black grubs with colored patches on their backs emerge.'"

They don't look much as if they will ever become ladybugs. But when Violet was brand-new she looked quite like a pink hairy monkey and not very much like herself, so it is possible, she thinks.

Nicola makes a long larva body out of wire and then strings on some grayish-black beads that look a lot like the little sections of the larva body in the encyclopedia. Using what is left of the nail polish after the spillage, Violet carefully paints the colored parts on. Then Nicola uses her pliers to make feelers for its head and little lumpy legs on either side of its body. Violet makes it another leaf to sit on. And that is stage two.

Stage three is the pupa stage.

"'A pupa is a sort of case that the larva curls up in while it grows and develops a bit more,'" reads Violet.

It is probably quite cozy inside a pupa, Violet thinks. Like being in a sleeping bag but with your head in too.

Pupae have almost the coloring of a ladybug, but they are much wrinklier on the outside. At first it seems quite tricky to make one. Nicola has a bead that is about the right shape (like a baked bean) but it is blue, which is not at all the right color. However, in her room, Violet has a collection of the little pieces of foil that chocolates are sometimes wrapped in. One of them is a sort of

rusty red, which is just the right color. Nicola wraps it around the bead and wrinkles it a bit. It is a perfect pupa and sits very well on another of Violet's felt leaves.

The final stage is the best one, Violet thinks.

"'The new ladybug emerges from the pupa, hardens, and begins to search for food.'"

It must be quite exciting to be a newly emerging ladybug, Violet thinks. A bit like coming out of a

dark movie
theater into
the busy daytime
world.

Nicola makes a round ladybug body out of tiny red beads all sewn next to each other, round and round, spotted with black ones. This takes the longest time of all, and Violet thinks that soon *she* may need to begin searching for food.

But as she watches Nicola cleverly forming the beaded ladybug with her tiny needle, Violet thinks again of Small Gloria and, as well as hungriness, she has the feeling of sadness inside her.

7

The Red Matchbox

When the beaded ladybug is finished, Violet and Nicola pin all the different stages of the life cycle of a ladybug onto velvet boards that Nicola made for displaying her earrings at the market. Underneath the velvet the boards are made of cork, so they are very good for pinning things to.

It is a good display, and Nicola has the look of someone who is

trying not to be too pleased, in case someone thinks that it is boasting. Violet does not think it is boasting. Violet thinks it is the most beautiful beaded life cycle of any creature that she has ever seen.

"Nicola," says Violet, "do you

still need that box?" She means the matchbox that Nicola usually keeps red beads in, but now they are all used up on stage four of the ladybug, so it is empty.

"I was going to put some more beads in it," says Nicola.

"Oh," says Violet.

Even though really it is just an ordinary matchbox, Nicola has covered it in red paper and added some glitter glue, and Violet quite likes it.

"What do you want it for?" asks Nicola.

"Well, I need to bury Small Gloria," says Violet in a quiet voice. "But I'm not sure what to bury her in."

Nicola has some little scraps of velvet left over from when she covered the corkboard. She folds one into a little pillow and tucks it inside the red matchbox.

"How's that?" she asks.

"It is perfect," says Violet.

Violet carefully tips up the jar that was Small Gloria's home. Into her hand fall the rainbowy glass pebble and the round body of Small Gloria. She lays them side by side on the velvet pillow.

"Where do you want to bury her?" asks Nicola.

"Under the fennel patch," says Violet. "It was her natural habitat."

Violet doesn't want to bury Small Gloria just yet. She would like to think of a suitable ceremony for the burial first. So she leaves the matchbox in Nicola's room while they have lunch.

After lunch Nicola needs a nap because she didn't sleep all night from worrying about the natural science fair. While Nicola is napping, Violet goes into her own room and writes a song for Small Gloria.

8
The Suitable Ceremony

By the time Nicola has woken up from her nap, Violet has decided on a suitable ceremony for the burial of Small Gloria.

"I don't think she would have wanted too much of a fuss," Violet explains to Nicola. "Just her family gathered around, who live in the fennel patch, anyway, and us, perhaps saying a few things and singing a song."

"You want me to come too?" asks Nicola.

"Well, even though you didn't know Small Gloria, you know all about ladybugs, and I think it would be nice."

"All right," says Nicola.

Violet has some red rain boots and she draws black spots on them with a marker, in honor of Small Gloria. Nicola has red spotty hair clips that Violet would like her to wear. Then they take the match-box outside into the garden, and the ceremony begins.

"I did not know Small Gloria for very long," says Violet, "but I expect that ever since she was hatched, she was a special sort of ladybug. It was not always easy to understand her. For example, she preferred aphids to cheese-on-toast. But even though I accidentally did not help her very much, she has helped me."

Violet pauses.

"Is there anything you would like to add, Nicola?"

At first Nicola cannot think of anything she would like to add. But then she says, "Actually, yes. I didn't know Small Gloria, but I am pretty sure that she knew Violet was actually try-ing to help her, not hurt her. Also, I would like to say that I am dedicating my natural science display to Small Gloria, wherever she is, because she gave a very helpful idea to Violet and Violet gave the idea to me."

Then they sing the song that Violet has written on a piece of paper, and it goes like this:

Being outside
where fennel is growing.
Munching on aphids,
the breeze
gently blowing.
Feeling the sun on
her red spotty wings.
These were a few
of Small Gloria's favorite
things.

Violet and Nicola bury the red matchbox in the fennel patch together with the folded-up piece of paper with the song on it, and Violet sends a good wish to the small ladybug.

And then it is done.

9
Honorable Mention

On Monday it is the Natural Science Fair, and families and friends are allowed to go and see it in the evening. So Mama, Vincent, Nicola,

Dylan, and Violet all go in the car to Nicola's school.

The fair is set up in the school hall on tables, one for each student, and their names are on little cards at the front. There are some very good projects, Violet thinks. Wayne

Killarney has grown a sort of bean plant in special see-through soil, so you can look at the roots as well as the top. Na-Kyoung Song has split the stem of a white rose and put each half into a different jar of water with food coloring in it, which has made the rose go half pink and half purple.

At the end of the evening, when everyone has had time to look at every single display in the fair, there will be a prize for the Greatest Contribution to Natural Science.

Violet hopes that Nicola will win it, and maybe she will, because lots of people are stopping to look at the beaded life cycle of the ladybug, and one lady is saying that stages one and two are pretty enough to wear as brooches.

At the bottom of Nicola's display

is a little card where she has written

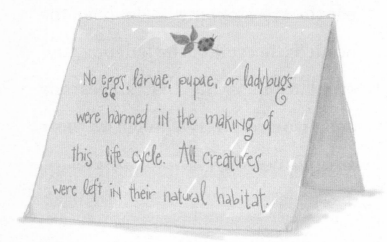

No eggs, larvae, pupae, or ladybugs
were harmed in the making of
this life cycle. All creatures
were left in their natural habitat.

And in very small writing on the
back of the card, where no one can
see, is written

in memory of small gloria

It is quite exciting when the time comes for the judging. There are three judges, and they have all been whispering in a serious way about who will get the prize, which is wrapped in gold paper on their desk. Everyone is quiet and some of the people in Nicola's class have

their fingers crossed behind their backs that they will be the winner of whatever is in the gold paper, which Violet suspects is a microscope. The only prize you get in Violet's class is a jelly bean for twenty-out-of-twenty in spelling. Violet thinks she would practice spelling more if things like microscopes were involved.

"The winner of this year's prize for the Greatest Contribution to Natural Science," begins the main judge, "is a student who has worked hard, thought creatively, and shown a great passion for this interesting subject."

Violet is sure that Nicola has worked hard and thought creatively, but she did say that natural science was worse than math—much worse. Perhaps that is not really showing a great passion. Violet feels quite nervous.

"So we are awarding the prize to . . ."

Violet crosses her toes in one of her shoes.

"Anson McGregor, for his ant farm and for his imaginative story entitled 'A Day in the Life of an Ant.'"

Even though Violet quite liked the story, she does not feel like clapping for Anson McGregor. But Mama quickly says you have to clap for everyone, even if they are not your sister, so Violet claps, anyway, but softly and for a short time.

When Anson McGregor opens

the prize, it is not a microscope. It is only a boxed copy of the same *Encyclopedia of Natural Science* that Nicola already has, which makes Violet feel a bit better about her not winning it.

Then the judge says, "However, we would also like to give an honorable mention to Nicola Mackerel for her beaded 'Life Cycle of the Ladybug,' because it was especially made leav-

ing all creatures in their natural habitat, which is the way natural science should be, wherever possible."

It is much more fun clapping for Nicola, and Violet does it loudly and for quite a long time.

The judge gives Nicola a special honorable mention bookmark with a tree frog on it.

And when they get home, Nicola gives it to Violet as a thank-you.

10 The Doughnut Crumbs

The next weekend Violet and Mama go to the shopping center again, as Mama needs some green wool that is on sale, and every person in the Mackerel family, plus Vincent, needs a new toothbrush, and Dylan wants some black hair dye, which is part of his stage.

When they are just about to go home they run into Mrs. Lin again, who is in the mood for a cup of tea.

"Would you mind?" Mama asks Violet. "I know it's been a long day already."

"I don't mind," says Violet.

So they go down to the food court.

"Please could I have a dough-nut?" asks Violet while Mama is buying the cups of tea.

Mama says she can, and Violet picks one that is still warm and has been rolled around in cinnamon and sugar.

She eats three-quarters of the
doughnut and, while Mama and Mrs.
Lin are saying, "Aren't there a lot

of commercials on television these days" and "There is hardly any time left for the actual television shows," Violet makes the last quarter into crumbs.

Soon the small brown sparrow flies down. Violet thinks that maybe he has remembered her because of the daisy dress thread, which is woven into his nest in the roof of the shopping center.

"I have something different for you today," says Violet, sprinkling the doughnut crumbs onto the floor. The sparrow hops and jumps just near where she is sitting, pecking at the crumbs and nibbling.

As she sprinkles, Violet thinks a bit more about the Theory of Helping Small Things, even though there isn't any particular help she needs today.

She wonders if the sparrow might like her to make him a soft nest in her room, perhaps in between the

boxes of puzzles on the bookshelves. She could listen to him chirping in the morning and bring him worms from the garden for breakfast.

Maybe the sparrow would like to have a bath with Violet so she could shampoo his feathers while Mama shampoos Violet's hair.

Just as Violet is wondering if the sparrow might even like to come to school with her, tucked safely in her schoolbag, she finds that she has stepped onto the mat in front of the big automatic doors of the food court.

They slide open and in a flash of feathery wings, the small brown sparrow flies out.

Violet watches him flutter up into the sky and swoop over toward the park, where there are trees and a small pond and lots of other sparrows too.

Violet waves good-bye a little sadly. It would have been fun to take the sparrow to school.

But it is nice to think that perhaps she has helped him find his way back to the place he lives and grows best.